PERCY JACKSON & THE OLYMPIANS

BOOK ONE

THE LIGHTNING THIEF

The Graphic Novel

by

RICK RIORDAN

Adapted by
Robert Venditti

Art by
Attila Futaki

Color by
José Villarrubia

Layouts by
Orpheus Collar

Lettering by
Chris Dickey

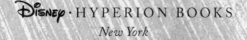

DISNEP·HYPERION BOOKS
New York

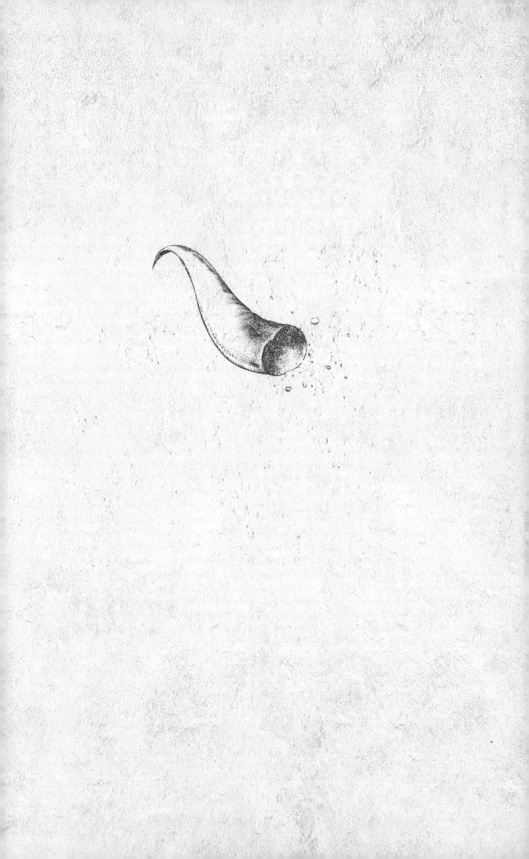

JUST EAST OF ST. LOUIS. JUNE 13.

8 DAYS UNTIL THE SUMMER SOLSTICE AND AN OLYMPIAN BATTLE ROYAL ENSUES.

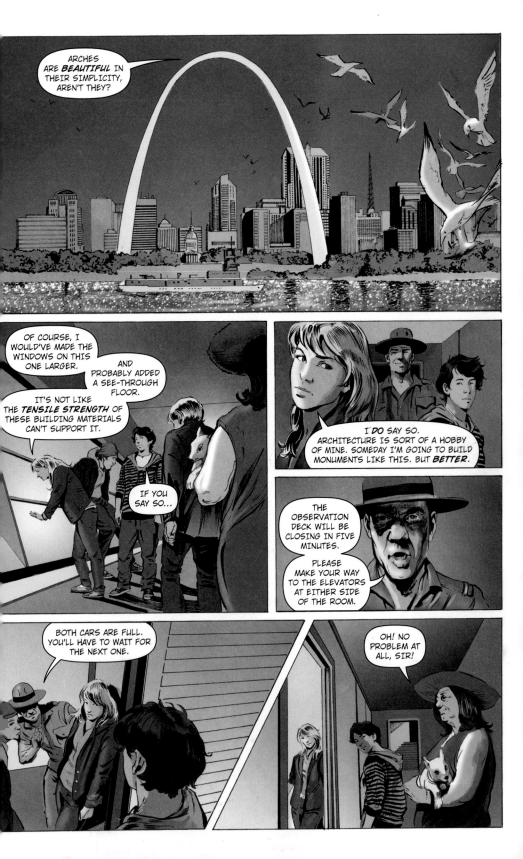

Adapted from the novel
Percy Jackson & the Olympians, Book One: The Lightning Thief

Text copyright © 2010 by Rick Riordan
Illustrations copyright © 2010 Disney Enterprises, Inc.

Design by Jim Titus
Edited by Christian Trimmer

Printed in the United States of America
V381-8386-5-13011
First Edition
10 9 8 7 6 5 4
ISBN 978-1-4231-1696-7 (hardcover)
Library of Congress Cataloging-in-Publication Data on file.
ISBN 978-1-4231-1710-0 (paperback)
Library of Congress Catalog Card Number on file.

Visit www.PercyJacksonBooks.com
and www.HyperionBooksForChildren.com